THE TYRELL SHOW
SEASON ONE

The Tyrell Show

Season One

Written by Miles Grose

Illustrated by Shaz Lym

SCHOLASTIC

Scholastic Australia
PO Box 579 Gosford NSW 2250
ABN 11 000 614 577
www.scholastic.com.au

Part of the Scholastic Group
Sydney • Auckland • New York • Toronto • London • Mexico City
• New Delhi • Hong Kong • Buenos Aires • Puerto Rico

Published by Scholastic Inc in 2022.
This edition published by Scholastic Australia in 2022.

Book design by Katie Fitch.
Cover art by Shaz Enrico Lym.
Interior artwork by Shaz Enrico Lym and
The Dizzy Devils with Artful Doodlers.

ISBN: 978-1-76129-372-6

Printed by McPherson's Printing Group, Maryborough, VIC.
Scholastic Australia's policy, in association with McPherson's Printing Group, is to use papers that are renewable and made efficiently from wood from responsibly managed sources, so as to minimise its environmental footprint.

22 23 24 25 26 / 2

For Vincent, Iris, and Judy—my dad, my mom, and my sister—
I am who I am because of them!
—MG

THE
TYRELL
SHOW

EPISODE ONE:
A WORD FROM OUR HOST

Good morning, everyone, and welcome to another season of *The Tyrell Show.* Why do I call it that? you ask. Because I'm Tyrell and this is my show . . . I guess. To all my regular listeners, I say, "Hey," and thanks for joining the livestream podcast that takes place in my head. And for all the new kids listening, thanks for joining me! And I do mean *kids* 'cause if you're an adult checking out my show, let me take this time to share something my mother taught me, "STRANGER DANGER!" There, I had to do that. *The Tyrell Show* is a safe place for me to share my thoughts on my life, and well, having some weird old adult I don't know listening in is definitely not cool.

Okay, glad I got that out of the way. Like I said, this is a new season of *The Tyrell Show.* The minute school was over last spring, I took the summer off from doing my podcast. I had a lot of fun! I went swimming in the neighborhood pool, which was great! Me and my friends only got kicked out four times, which is way better than last year, when we got kicked out twelve times. I guess following the rules is a good thing. Still, I never laughed harder than when my best friend, Boogie, belly flopped into the pool next to Monique. She SCREAMED at him! It was hilarious! We got kicked out for that, and if I'm being honest, I hope we get kicked

out for the same thing next summer. Like I said before, Boogie is my best friend, AND he's kind of a giant, so his splash was epic! He should do it every year. It could be like a big party with food and rides and fireworks . . . we could sell tickets. It would be amazing! If he does it again next summer, I promise to do a special episode of my show so that you can at least hear the splash.

EPISODE TWO:
ALL ABOUT ME AND MY PODCAST

Okay, where was I? Oh yeah, so, like, if you've never listened to my podcast before, I guess I should tell you a little bit about it. On my show, I talk about a lot of important stuff like playing and school and pizza and smelly things, but mostly I talk about me and the people in my life. And you can join me as I share my show in my head while I'm daydreaming, which is pretty much the only place where my sister, Al, can't bother me.

Also I have guests on my show sometimes, only they don't know they're on. Sometimes when they're talking to me I let you hear everything they're saying. Other times I might even imagine something they said and let you hear that too! But really, like I said before, pretty much no one knows about my show . . . except for my best friend, Boogie. He thinks he's my cohost, but really, between you and me, he's not; he's just a special guest. I mean, when you think about it, how would I even let him into my head's recording studio? Maybe through my ear, but unless someone invents a shrinking device I'm guessing that would hurt.

Anyway, I share what it's like for me at home with my family and out in my neighborhood with my friends and even sometimes when I'm in school. Oh, and every now and then, I do "special episodes," like last summer when I did an episode from Disney World! My sister, Al, threw up on Space Mountain, funnel cake and fruit punch everywhere—that was amazing! Hopefully that episode will win an award. And this season I'll be sharing my adventures as I start the sixth grade at Marcus Garvey Elementary. Oh, and not to brag, especially 'cause my dad says I shouldn't, but sixth grade is a pretty big deal—it means I'm one of the big kids now. Us sixth graders are the oldest in the school, and the young kids are probably going to be looking up to us. I'm a little nervous about that. I don't know if you know, but being eleven and a half years old is really hard, and sometimes I worry about a lot of things: Do people like me? Am I safe? What will I be when I grow up? Did Tricia hear me fart in science class? Yup, my show tackles the tough issues that kids like me face each day.

Oh, and I almost forgot . . . the big sixth-grade show! What's that? you ask. Only the most important event ever! It's a show that the sixth graders in our school put on every year right at the end of the first semester. Each year the school comes up with a new theme for the show that's supposed to kind of send out a positive message for our futures. I heard this year's theme is going to be "New Beginnings." I don't actually know what that means, but if I'm being honest, it sounds a little boring.

Last year the theme was "The Fast and the Future," and a lot of the kids dressed up like fast cars and tried to talk like Vin Diesel. It was awesome! I think some of the parents were not very happy with it though, so I guess this year they wanted to make sure the show wouldn't be as fun.

No matter what the theme is I'm excited because ever since I was a little kid I have always wanted to have a big role in the sixth-grade show. Why? you ask. I've gotta say you ask a lot of questions, but if you must know, one reason is that it's kind of a way for sixth graders to leave their mark before they go on to their next school.

They hang pictures of some of the kids from the play around the hallways, and they post videos of the performance online. One time, the news even came to the school and did a story about it, and two of the kids got in a video that went viral. Basically what I'm saying is that it's the most important thing ever! And another reason I want to do it—and don't tell anyone this—is because I'm kind of shy. I mean, I really believe that I would love to perform and have everyone yelling my name and calling me "amazing," but then when I actually think about doing it and really picture it, being up there onstage, I get nervous. But this year I'm going to overcome my fear and get a huge part and have a fan club and get a bunch of followers online. You'll see.

Hey, I just thought about it, most of you new listeners don't really know a lot about me. My dad says it's rude to not introduce yourself when you first meet someone, so I guess I should do that now. My name is Tyrell Edwards, and I think I told you already, but just in case, I'm eleven and a half years old. I think that makes me a tween or at least a pre-tween. I'm not shaving yet, but I keep checking my face for hair—probably gonna come any day now.

Dad calls to me.

That voice you just heard is my dad . . . really, I didn't imagine it. He calls me High Speed, which is cool, I guess, only most people think it's 'cause I'm fast . . . I'm really not! Not at all, I'm actually

mad slow, I mean "very" slow . . . my mom hates when I speak using slang instead of the proper words—sorry, Mom! Where was I? Oh yeah, slow. When new kids meet me and hear my nickname, they always want to race me, and no matter how many times I tell them they're faster than me, we still wind up racing and they wind up beating me and saying, "You ain't fast!"

I did win one race though. One time this kid said he could beat me even if he ran backward, which I told him was dangerous,

which he didn't believe, which then ended badly when he ran into a pole. If I'm being honest, I have to say he was way ahead of me when he ran into that pole. My dad said, "Hey, a win is a win!" So like I said, I did win a race once.

By the way when it comes to the whole "always be honest" thing, my dad says, "Honesty is the best policy, except when your mom asks you about her cooking." So to be honest, when it comes to being honest, I'm a little confused. Honestly, I blame my mom and dad for that. Oh yeah, and speaking of my dad, I never told you why he gave me the nickname High Speed.

He said it was because whenever he asked me a question like "What's the capital of New York?" (Albany) or "How far are we away from the sun?" (between ninety two and ninety four million miles, depending on the time of the year), I answered so quickly it was like I was a high-speed internet connection. I guess that was my dad's way of saying I'm smart. The fact is I've always kind of been smart, but being smart doesn't always feel good. Sometimes it feels like no matter what I do, my parents and teachers expect me to do better. A lot of my friends think that I think I'm better than them. That makes me sad—I mean, I just want to be treated like I'm a normal eleven-and-a-half-year-old, but I know that's theoretically impossible . . . sorry for the big word; I use them when I get nervous.

Speaking of nervous, I have to go to the bathroom, so I'll need to end this episode. Trust me, you don't want to come into the bathroom with me. But come back, today is a pretty big day for me. It's the first day of school and I'm already a little stressed out, so really, come back . . . seriously. I'll only be a minute unless Al needs to use the bathroom, in which case I might take a little longer. Okay, talk to you soon!

EPISODE THREE:
MEET MY FAMILY

Hey, everyone. You know earlier I told you all about me, but I didn't mention anything about my amazing family, and, like, that's not cool, so here goes.

My mom's name is Charlene Edwards, and she's thirty-seven, but please don't tell her I told you that. I'm serious! She likes to pretend she's a little younger, and on her birthday whenever any of us make a mistake and say her real age, well, she makes this really scary face, like reeeally scary. I'm just saying it's not something you ever want to see. Anyway, when she's not making that face, she's really pretty and she's extremely nice for an old person, I mean *older* person. She's a social worker, which means she helps people. I think that's a great job for her because she always helps me, my sister, and my dad with just about everything. When we're sick, she knows just what to give us to make us feel better. And whenever we mess up, she knows exactly what to yell, I mean to say, to set us straight. And, um, about her cooking . . . everything is so flavorful and delicious, especially her famous oatmeal raisin garlic cookies. There, that's done. It's always good to say nice things about people, plus my dad gives me and my sister fifty cents every time we compliment her food. Really, I don't know why she puts garlic in them. She always kind of adds in one thing that shouldn't be there whenever she's cooking. With her special cookies, she says, "Garlic is good for you." I don't know if it's good for me, but I know it's not good for a cookie. Um, so I'm not saying my mom can't cook at all. She does make good cereal—I mean, she pours the right amount of milk in the bowl in proportion to the cornflakes. Sorry for the big word, I just got a little stressed again. Then there's:

My dad, Edward Edwards. Ha! Isn't that funny? His first name is almost his last name. That used to confuse me way back when I was a little kid. I thought everyone's first name was their last name. In kindergarten, I told my teacher my name was Tyrell Tyrells. She laughed and my best friend, Boogie, said I cried, but I don't remember doing that; plus, Boogie makes things up. I'll tell you more about Boogie later; right now I'm talking about my dad. He is tall, and strong, and has a beard, like LeBron James, which is why I know my beard is on the way. He's also thirty-seven years old, but he doesn't mind me saying that. And he's a bus driver, or "bus captain" as he calls it. I've been on his bus, and I think he looks pretty cool sitting in his bus captain's chair, like he's in charge. I want to be in charge of something one day. My dad is easy to talk to and always has great advice. And even if I don't always understand what he's saying, I just like the sound of his voice. Sometimes he'll be talking to me and the next thing I know I'll wake up in my bed. I'm not saying my dad is boring, I'm saying his voice has the magical power of sleep with maybe just a touch of boring sprinkled in, which is okay 'cause I love sprinkles.

Ugh . . . then there's . . . *don-don-don*:

There's my sister. She's fifteen and sooooo annoying. Her friends call her Alex, short for Alexandra, which she likes. I call her Al short for Alfred, which she hates. She bullies me, and I tell on her, kind of standard older-sister, younger-brother stuff. People say she's pretty, but I don't see it. Boogie says she's "gorgeous," but Boogie also loves my mom's cooking. She's always getting yelled at for being on her phone. My dad told her that if she doesn't stop staring down at her phone all day, eventually her neck will stay curved forever. To me that's strange because she has a really long neck and long eyelashes, so that just makes me think she'll grow up to be a giraffe. I told that to Boogie, and he said he thinks giraffes are adorable. She can be funny sometimes though, especially when she tells Boogie to get away from her. And, if I'm being honest, I really do like her. I can't say "love" though because, from what I've seen on the reality TV shows she watches, love comes with too much drama.

TYRELL! WHAT ARE YOU DOING IN THERE? DO YOU SEE THE TIME? YOU DON'T WANT TO BE LATE FOR YOUR FIRST DAY OF SIXTH GRADE. NOW GET YOUR BUTT MOVING!
MOM! LANGUAGE, PLEASE!
EXCUSE ME?
UM, NOTHING. BE RIGHT OUT!
YOU READY FOR YOUR FIRST DAY, YOUNG MAN?
YES.
ALL RIGHT. WELL, YOU HEARD YOUR MOM, GET YOUR HIGH-SPEED BUTT MOVING!
OKAY, DAD.

Sorry about that *butt* thing. Like I said, my parents don't know when they're on my show, or even know about my show at all. Wow, I really lost track of time. There are some other people I wanted to tell you about, but I'll have to do that later. Anyway, I had better get going. I don't want to be late on my first day. I'm going to end this episode now, but tune back in in a little bit and catch me on my way to school.

EPISODE FOUR:
ARE YOU READY FOR SCHOOL?

Thanks for coming back! Right now I'm on my way to school, and as you can see if you could actually see, which you can't, but please try to imagine, I'm here at my favorite bodega. If you don't know what that is, it's like a little supermarket where you can buy things you need. As a treat, sometimes my parents give me money to buy lunch to take to school, which is AMAZING! Why did I get so excited when I said "AMAZING"? Well, partly because the nice man who owns the place, Hector, makes . . . THE . . . BEST . . . sandwiches! And partly because my mom usually makes my lunch and . . . well you know the rest. Come meet Hector; he's nice even if he does smell like pickles.

HECTOR'S
DELI · GROCERY · ATM · TROPICAL PRODUCE
COFFEE
HEY, YOU READY FOR YOUR FIRST DAY BACK AT SCHOOL, LITTLE MAN? THE USUAL?
YES, PLEASE. VEGAN TURKEY AND CHEESE PLEASE.

Right now if you could see me, you would see I'm staring directly at an imaginary camera with a look of shock, "Are you ready for school"? Seriously? I mean, is there a worse question you could ask a kid on his first day back? Does he know what he just asked me? He might as well have said, *"Are you ready for summer to be over?" "Are you ready for fun to end?" "Are you ready for homework and tests?"* What is it with adults? If they like school so much, why don't they go and let us go to work. For real, if Hector didn't make the best vegan-turkey-and-cheese sandwich in the world, I might have to think about going across the street to the other bodega that smells like cats. Look, I'm going to grab my sandwich, some chips, and a drink, boring stuff. So I'll meet you all outside.

EPISODE FIVE:
BOOGIE

Got my sandwich, now what can I talk to you about? Oh yeah, so the other day me and Boogie were watching this hysterical cartoon on YouTube with this purple cow that was wearing a jet pack . . .

Yeah, that's my BF, Boogie, and like I said, he's the best and all, but he is a not a good storyteller and right now he is *ruining* that cartoon. Don't believe me? Listen:

See? Anyway that's Boogie, he's almost always on my show. And sure he tells terrible stories, but he gives great advice! I guess this is a good time for me to tell you a little bit more about Boogie:

I met Boogie on my first day of kindergarten. All I remember was that he was really big, not chubby, just big. Everyone was scared of him at first, but one day at lunch, he came up to me

DEREK LACEY aka BOOGIE: MY BEST FRIEND

and offered me half his sandwich. That was the first and last time I ever ate tuna fish . . . yuck! Did you know that tuna fish salad is made out of actual mushed-up fish and mayonnaise? If you know about that stuff, please don't give my mom the recipe 'cause I know she'll make it! Plus, she'll probably add chocolate chips! Anyway, he handed it to me, and it smelled terrible! I didn't want to eat it, but I didn't want to make the nice giant mad, so I took one bite, then made a face and spit it out! I looked at him to see if he was angry, but he was just laughing. He laughed so hard that a booger flew out of his nose. Everyone was like, "Illll!" and I was like, "Uh-oh," but he didn't get upset, he just put some boogers on his finger and started chasing us. Everyone was running, yelling,

"Boogie Boogie Boogie," even the giant! When the game was over, our teacher, Mrs. Karg, made him wash his hands and then took us back to class. From that day on, the kids in the class would ask him if we could play "Boogie," and he would just smile, dig up his nose, and chase us. After a while, we just started calling him *Boogie*, and just like a booger you flick on someone's back, it stuck. Now that's the true story, but if you ask Boogie how he got the name, he'll tell you he's got dance moves, which he doesn't . . . and that some high school kid he had a dance battle with gave him the nickname, which is ridiculous. But that's kind of why Boogie is my best friend—he's silly and funny and just the best person to be around. Like I said, he's really *big*, big like in our class pictures

people think he's the teacher. As big as he is though, he never bullies anyone and the only time he gets angry is when someone messes with me. He's got my back and I've got his. He always says if we were a superhero team, he would be a big robot and I would be inside his head telling him what to do. I kind of like that 'cause I like robots. But if I'm being honest, to me Boogie is a superhero all by himself, just a goofy one.

If you're wondering, he's still talking about the cartoon, and if I'm being honest as I listen to him, I'm starting to think Boogie's version is funnier, strange but funnier. Maybe he's not such a bad storyteller after all. Anyway, I better get back to listening to him; if I don't nod sometimes, he usually figures out I'm not paying attention. I don't want to be rude. You don't have to listen though—actually I think it's a good time for a commercial break. Feel free to get some snacks. My mom gives me stuff like carrot sticks, but if you can go and get a cookie or something like that, I promise I won't tell. See you when I get to school!

EPISODE SIX:
TAKE A DEEP BREATH

And we're back! What kind of snack did you get? I hope it was something good and gooey or even better, something sour! I love candy or even fruits that make my face pucker up, like green apples or lemons! Anyway, I'm now standing in front of Marcus Garvey Elementary. This has been my school for six years. A lot of memories! I remember the time I fell down the back staircase and broke my wrist. And I remember the time I slipped in the schoolyard and twisted my ankle. Then there was the time I got food poisoning in the lunchroom from the fish sticks. Gee, what a dangerous place!

Really though, I owe a lot to MGE, that's what we call Marcus Garvey Elementary. Did you know that Marcus Garvey was an important Black civil rights leader and that he founded the Universal Negro Improvement Association and African Communities League? Pretty special person.

I don't think I've ever stopped and really looked at my school before. Wow! After this year it's not even going to be my school anymore! That's deep. It's kind of making me sad, but I'm not going to think about it like that. Nope! I'm a sixth grader now! Practically grown! And I'm about to pretty much be in charge of this school and be the star of the sixth-grade show!

WE'RE ABOUT TO BE IN CHARGE OF THIS SCHOOL, BOOGIE!
YEAH! WAIT, WHAT ABOUT THE PRINCIPAL? ISN'T SHE STILL IN CHARGE?
YES, TECHNICALLY, BUT OTHER THAN HER...
AND OUR TEACHERS?
YEAH, AND THE TEACHERS BUT...
AND THE SECURITY GUARDS AND THE LUNCH LADIES AND THE CUSTODIANS, OH, AND JAMAL AND HIS CREW AND ALL THE OTHER BAD KIDS AND...
YOU MADE YOUR POINT.

Leave it to Boogie for a reality check. Uh-oh, it's getting late. Time to start the sixth grade. It's a big step. Whenever I'm nervous, my dad says, "Take a deep breath, then take a moment to think about what you need to do, take another deep breath, and then just do it." My dad is really smart, maybe even a little smarter than me.

I have a feeling this is going to be the greatest year of my life. I would invite you in, but I think I need to handle today on my own. Talk to you soon!

EPISODE SEVEN:
WE'LL SEE

Hey, thanks for waiting for me. I bet you're wondering how my first day was? If I'm being honest, it wasn't like what I thought it would be. Have you ever been looking forward to something that one of your friends told you about? They bragged about it and said, "It's amazing . . . you'll see!" but then you didn't see? Well, it was kind of like that. I thought the teachers would be extra nice to us and the younger kids would give us gifts like candy or offer to do our homework or something. I had even heard that the principal was going to call all the sixth graders into her office and give us a special award, but nope, nothing. Boogie told me that one so I should've known. I'm sure things will get better

though; I guess we'll see. Oh, and UGH . . . I have to sit next to Shelly! For the whole year! Do you believe that? Shelly has been like my mortal enemy since first grade. Why? you ask. For one she calls me *Ty-Smell*. Okay that's not my name and it's not even close to funny. To get back at her, I call her *Smell-ey* . . . now *that's* funny. On the positive side, they made an announcement about auditions for the sixth-grade show. If I'm being honest, just hearing them talk about the auditions made me nervous. Anyway, I wonder where Boogie is? He's not in my class, so I haven't seen him since this morning. I wonder how his day went. I can't seem to find Boogie. That's okay though because there's one thing I've learned hanging around Boogie, if you don't find him, he finds you.

GUESS WHO?
A GIANT CHEESE SNACK?
NO, IT'S ME, BOOGIE! *HAHAHA!*
YES, I KNEW THAT, BUT YOUR HANDS SMELL LIKE CHEESE.
OH YEAH, YOU'RE RIGHT. I DID HAVE SOME CHEESE PUFFS THIS MORNING.
THIS MORNING?! THAT'S DISGUSTING! YOUR FINGERS ARE GOING TO WIND UP STAYING ORANGE, LIKE ERNIE ON *SESAME STREET*.
ANYWAY, HOW WAS SCHOOL?

IT WAS GOOD. MY TEACHER, MR. MACK, COULDN'T OPEN HIS DESK SO HE STARTED PULLING ON THE DRAWER REALLY HARD AND THEN ALL OF A SUDDEN HIS THINGS FLEW OUT AND PAPERS WENT EVERYWHERE SO HE STARTED YELLING AND...

I wish I could be like Boogie—little things make him so happy. If I'm being honest, so far this day has me feeling a little down. I'm not going to lie; the more I think about it, the more I'm really disappointed by my first day. It wasn't as special as I thought it was going to be. On top of that, as each minute goes by, I get more and more nervous about the audition. And it doesn't help that right now I kind of smell like artificial cheese. Normally a Hector sandwich for lunch and a Boogie story would cheer me up, but today I need something special. Would you guys like to meet my dog, Monty? Well, he's not actually mine—he lives at the animal shelter—but my parents said that if I do good in school this year, help out around the house, and am . . . a little nicer to Al, they'll consider letting me adopt him. Honestly, the first two will be easy, but being nicer to Al will be tough. I'm going to really try though because Monty is the best! And I think seeing him will help me feel a little better. So you wanna come with? I'm going to assume you said yes. Let me tell Boogie—I know he'll be happy to go.

EPISODE EIGHT:
MONTY

Well, we're here at Paws and Claws. There's Mrs. Wilkins, she's the nice person who runs the place. She says I can call her Judy, but my parents always tell me it's rude to call an adult by their first name. Let's say hi.

WHAT? OH NO, I'M LEAVING!
SHE'S JUST JOKING, BOOGIE. RIGHT, MRS. WILKINS?
OF COURSE I AM. DEREK, CALI CAT JUST ADORES YOU.
REALLY?
SO MONTY CAN TALK?
REALLY! OH AND TYRELL, MONTY HAS BEEN ASKING FOR YOU.
NO, DEREK, THAT'S JUST A FIGURE OF SPEECH.

NO NEED TO BE AFRAID, DEREK—SHE JUST WANTS TO PLAY WITH YOU.

Mrs. Wilkins takes off after Boogie.

Yup . . . Boogie's really afraid of cats, and Cali Cat knows it. She chases him every time we're here.

And there's Monty! Wanna meet him? I'll introduce you.

As you already know, Monty lives in an animal shelter. Most days me and Boogie go there and play with all the dogs and some of the cats. I say *some of the cats* because cats are a little strange, plus Boogie is really afraid of them. He even runs from kittens—it's hilarious! Mrs. Wilkins says that the animals always look forward to us coming. Anyway, ever since the first time I went there, me and Monty had a connection. I know Mrs. Wilkins said she was joking when she said he could talk, but the truth is he can.

When he first came to the shelter, he didn't have a name tag, so no one knew what to call him. I looked him right in the eyes and asked him his name, and he barked, and it soooo sounded like he said, "Monty." I told Mrs. Wilkins so now that's what everyone calls him. Anyway, Monty is an English bulldog who slobbers a lot, loves to play, and, like I said, can bark his own name. I really, really hope I get to adopt him one day because Monty is great and he needs a home! Oh, and if you live anywhere near the Paws and Claws animal shelter or any animal shelter, you should think about asking your parents if you can go there and adopt a pet because really they all need homes, even that one strange cat with a white patch of fur around his eyes. He's not so bad—I just think he has anger issues. Anyway, here he is. Everyone, say hi to Monty. Monty barked, not sure if you can hear him!

Did you hear that? He said, "Nice to meet you" in dog language. I'm so happy to see him! I can't wait to tell him all about my day.

Hahahaha! Cali Cat isn't giving up! Anyway I know I didn't tell you a lot about my first day. If I'm being honest, I think it's kind of got me down. I know it was only the first day and I guess things will get better, but I still feel kind of sad. You ever feel sad

and not really know why? My mom always says that when I get this way, I should stop and take time to think about how I feel and then try to figure out what's making me feel that way. Normally when I'm in a mood like this, I talk to my parents or I play with Boogie . . .

But right now I think Boogie has his own problems, like being chased by a cat! I'm probably going to take this time to talk to Monty about it. He's a really good listener, and he almost never interrupts unless, of course, if he has to poop. I promise to tell you all more about my day later. Right now I had better go and help Boogie.

Wow! And he called for his mommy, hilarious! This place definitely cheered me up! Talk to you all soon!

SOMEONE PLEASE SAVE ME!

STOP RUNNING. BOOGIE, YOU MIGHT HURT YOURSELF.

EPISODE NINE:
SIPPY SIPPY DRINK DRINK

Good morning, everyone. I'm standing outside waiting for Boogie and his little brother, Ricky. Before they show up, I think it would be best if I told you a little about Ricky.

Ricky is Boogie's little four-year-old brother, and he is so spoiled! You ever put a container of milk in your bookbag and then forgot about it? Like all day? I mean you forgot, like you didn't remember to drink it at lunch and then went out to play and then went back to class and then school ended and you went out to play some more and then you went home and then you grabbed your bookbag so that you could do your homework and then you looked inside and saw the milk and then smelled it? That type of spoiled! I'm not saying he smells like spoiled milk, I'm saying he *is* spoiled milk. Plus I'm lactose intolerant, so that doesn't help. It's Boogie's mom's fault. She calls him her "Sweet Little Pretty Ricky!" Other than that though, Boogie's mom is pretty great—she's like my second mom. She always has time to talk to me about anything, and she's kind of funny. She's a nurse, which probably explains why she's so nice because my mom told me that nurses take care of people. If you're wondering about Boogie's dad, he was a really brave soldier, and I think he died protecting us. I don't ask Boogie too much about him because I know it makes him sad. Since he's not around, Boogie has to help out a lot around the house, and in my opinion, his worst job is looking after Ricky. Most days we have to pick him up from day care, which is awful because he's usually cranky. OH YEAH, and Ricky always wants to do kiddy things like ride on the swing or play hide-and-seek . . . I mean, really, I'm eleven and a half. I don't have time for that stuff. Plus, he gets so dirty! It's like he looks for dirt to fall in. And then when we bring him home all dirty, we get in trouble! I can't wait until Ricky grows up or moves out or something.

Umm . . . so some of you might remember that from last season when I was in the fifth grade. I went after my dream of trying out for the school basketball team. And I did it for two reasons: They get to wear cool uniforms, and they get to play in front of big crowds who cheer loudly. Well, what I remember from the big day is that as I was changing into my basketball clothes I realized two things: One, I've never played basketball except in video games. And two, big crowds make me nervous. All of a sudden I started feeling really scared and I thought about just leaving and not trying out, but then I pictured my mom and dad being really disappointed and I also pictured Al making fun of me. With all that in my head, I decided to just go out and do my best.

ARE YOU TELLING YOUR AUDIENCE ABOUT IT NOW?
YES.
MY MOM'S HERE. SHE SAID SHE WOULD DROP US AT SCHOOL AFTER SHE DROPS RICKY AT DAY CARE.
SIPPY SIPPY DRINK DRINK SIPPY SIPPY DRINK!
THAT WAS EPIC! DID YOU TELL THEM HOW YOU WERE SO NERVOUS THAT YOU PUT YOUR SHOES ON THE WRONG FEET?

HI, RICKY.
RED AND BLUE AND EVEN PINK!
WHAT'S WRONG WITH HIM?
I DON'T KNOW. HE'S BEEN SINGING THAT ANNOYING SONG ALL WEEK—MAYBE HE'S BROKEN. DID YOU TELL YOUR AUDIENCE HOW YOU GOT CONFUSED ON THE COURT AND PUT THE BALL IN THE OTHER TEAM'S BASKET...

NO.
AND WHEN YOU'RE DONE WITH YOUR SIPPY SIPPY DRINK!
THREE TIMES!
NO! AND WILL BOTH OF YOU PLEASE STOP?!
I'M REALLY NERVOUS ABOUT THE AUDITION, AND I'M AFRAID WHAT HAPPENED LAST YEAR AT THE TRYOUTS IS GOING TO HAPPEN AT THE AUDITION.
I DON'T THINK THEY'RE GONNA MAKE YOU SHOOT ANY BASKETS.
STOP BEING FUNNY, BOOGIE, YOU KNOW WHAT I MEAN.

OF COURSE I DO. EVERYBODY GETS NERVOUS OR SCARED SOMETIMES. THAT'S NORMAL. LIKE MY MOM ALWAYS SAYS, "NEVER BE AFRAID TO FACE YOUR FEARS."

THANKS, BOOGIE.
YOU'RE WEL—ILL!

YUCK! HE JUST LICKED MY HAND!
WE HAD BETTER GO MEET YOUR MOM.

Um, BOOGIE...DID YOU KNOW YOUR SHOES ARE ON THE WRONG FEET?

NOT AGAIN! NOW THAT'S HILARIOUS!
MAKE SURE YOU PUT IT IN THE KITCHEN KITCHEN SINK!
YES, IT IS! THANKS, BOOGIE!

EPISODE TEN:
A SANDWICH

Good morning, everyone. It's been a long time since my last show. I could make up some excuse as to why I haven't done one in a while, like my brain microphone was broken or the people who write my show stopped coming to work, but all that would just be lies and not even good ones. First of all, I write my show in my head all by myself, and for all the time that I spend in my head, I've never actually seen a "brain microphone." If I'm being honest, the real reason I haven't done a show is that I've felt a little sad about the sixth grade. I also felt a little mad but mostly sad. Still not sure why though; I guess it's 'cause it's not what I expected it to be. I don't have a lot of really good friends in my class, and even more than that I don't feel any different. I thought I would feel older, like more grown-up, but I don't. Still, I'm really not completely sure why I feel sad, but I do know for a fact that I do feel mostly sad. How do I know I've been feeling mostly sad? you ask. Because the other day my mother made me a peanut butter, jelly, marshmallow, and turkey bacon sandwich . . . my favorite! Why she thought to add turkey bacon to it I'll never understand, but it's the one time that her extra ingredient is just perfect! She almost never makes that for me because she says it's not healthy, but she made it because she could tell I was sad and she thought it would cheer me up. Normally it would, but I don't know, I guess I just wasn't in the mood to feel better. Messed-up thing is that she brought it up to my room . . . *my room*! She pretty much never lets me eat in my room! She put it on my desk and said:

Okay, before you make fun of me for saying "*I love you too, Mommy,*" I only said all that "Mommy" stuff for her. Okay?! Now I'm not saying I don't love my mom—of course I do—but I'm getting too old for all that mushy "I love you" stuff, but I know she likes it and, well, she did make me my favorite and bring it all the way to my room, so it was the least I could do.

Anyway, back to that sandwich. Normally that salty peanut butter mixed with the sweet jelly, gooey marshmallow, and yummy bacon would automatically cheer me up, but it didn't. That delicious sandwich just sat there calling my name.

YOU ARE, BUT RIGHT NOW I'M NOT IN THE MOOD FOR YOU, SO PLEASE JUST SHUT YOUR BREAD!
WELL, I'M SORRY. I DIDN'T MEAN TO UPSET YOU.
NO, I'M SORRY, MR. SANDWICH, I MEAN SANDY, BUT RIGHT NOW A DELICIOUS SANDWICH IS NOT THE SOLUTION TO MY PROBLEMS.
SOUNDS LIKE YOU'RE UPSET ABOUT SOMETHING.
YEAH. SCHOOL. I THOUGHT THIS YEAR WAS GOING TO BE SPECIAL BUT IT'S NOT.
I'M SORRY TO HEAR THAT. THAT MUST BE VERY DISAPPOINTING. WHAT CAN YOU DO TO CHANGE THAT? IS THERE SOMETHING IN SCHOOL YOU COULD GET INVOLVED IN?

TYRELL, IF THERE'S ONE THING THAT I'VE LEARNED BEING A SANDWICH IS THAT YOU CAN BE ANYTHING. LOOK AT ME, I COULD'VE BEEN A HAM SANDWICH OR AN EGG SALAD SANDWICH OR, AS MUCH AS IT WOULD'VE HURT, A GRILLED CHEESE SANDWICH. I COULD'VE BEEN ANYTHING, BUT IN THE END I BECAME EXACTLY WHAT YOU WANTED ME TO BE, AND SO CAN YOU.
MAYBE YOU'RE RIGHT, SANDY. I THINK I WILL TRY OUT FOR THE SHOW! THANKS!
GLAD I COULD HELP. NOW, ONE LAST THING.
WHAT? OH YEAH!

Okay, if I'm being honest, I didn't really have a conversation with my sandwich. I mean if I did the last part would have ended with the sandwich screaming in pain as I ate it.

The truth is my dad came into my room a little later and talked to me. He was the one who told me that I could be anything I want to be. That sandwich didn't say anything to me, which is good because that would've just been scary. I will say, later that day after I ate it, Sandy was definitely talking in my stomach, and most of what it was saying was pretty bad. I think it sat out too long.

EPISODE ELEVEN:
YOU NEED A GOOD BREAKFAST

Hey, everyone, today is an exciting episode! I'm finally about to try out for the sixth-grade show. I have been practicing and practicing, and I think—no, I know—I am ready for my big audition. Well, I had better get this day started right with a good breakfast. Meet you at the kitchen table.

If I'm being honest, all that talk about me not being nervous made me nervous. And did you hear my family's reaction to me singing my own song? I think it's an amazing idea, don't you? My song, my feelings, my thoughts out there for everyone to hear. Hmm, now that I say that out loud it doesn't sound as good as I thought. I mean, what if they don't like it? And what if they start

DON'T ASK HIM THAT, EDWARD. IF HE'S NOT NERVOUS ALREADY, SAYING THAT WORD IS BOUND TO MAKE HIM NERVOUS.
SO THIS IS THE BIG DAY, HUH, HIGH SPEED? YOU NERVOUS?
HE'S DEFINITELY NERVOUS! I BET HE MESSES UP JUST LIKE HE DID WITH THE BASKETBALL TRYOUTS!

SHUT UP, AL!
THAT'S ENOUGH, TYRELL. DON'T TALK TO YOUR SISTER LIKE THAT.
YEAH, DON'T TALK TO YOUR SISTER LIKE THAT!

AND THAT'S ENOUGH OUT OF YOU, TOO, ALEXANDRA.
SO WHAT ARE YOU GOING TO DO FOR YOUR AUDITION?
I'M GOING TO SING.
HA!
ALEX, SERIOUSLY?! WHAT IS WRONG WITH YOU? WHY DON'T YOU TRY BEING SUPPORTIVE OF YOUR BROTHER?
AND WHAT ARE YOU GOING TO SING, HIGH SPEED?

MOM, DAD, AREN'T YOU GONNA SAY SOMETHING TO ALEX?
YES.
NO, I THINK I'M GOING TO ALLOW THAT ONE. TYRELL, DO YOU REALLY THINK THAT'S THE BEST IDEA? I MEAN. IT TAKES EVEN EXPERIENCED SONGWRITERS A WHILE TO DEVELOP A NEW SONG? DO YOU THINK YOURS IS READY?
HA!
OF COURSE IT IS. I'VE LISTENED IN ON HIM PRACTICING IT IN THE BATHROOM.
MOM!
AND MY BABY SOUNDED WONDERFUL! YOU GO ON AHEAD AND CLAIM YOUR PART IN THAT SHOW. YOU HEAR ME?

WELL, I CAN'T ARGUE WITH THAT. NOW FINISH UP—I'M GOING TO DROP YOU AT SCHOOL TODAY. BIG FUTURE STARS LIKE YOU SHOULDN'T HAVE TO WALK.

HA!
AND NO MATTER WHAT, JUST KNOW I LOVE YOU.
HA!
AND WHATEVER YOU DO, DON'T GET NERVOUS. HA!

to judge me and even boo me?! Okay, Tyrell, get that thought out of your head. Just believe in yourself . . . which by the way is the title of the song, "Just Believe in Yourself." A little corny, I know, but the first song I had was called "Pepperoni Pizza with a Salad on the Side," and the truth is, after you got past the chorus, it didn't make a lot of sense. Anyway, gotta go because right now I'm in the back seat of my dad's car with my dad and he's talking to me about something and it just looks like I'm ignoring him. Talk to you at the audition!

EPISODE TWELVE:
THE AUDITION

Well, I'm here. I'm not going to say I'm feeling nervous, but I will say, "Shut up, Al!" And I hope wherever she is she heard me . . . don't tell my parents I said that though. Now, I won't be able to talk to you as much because we have to be quiet in school, but I am going to leave my brain microphone on so that you can hear everything, maybe even my audition. I'll try to check in with you when I can, and really, thank you all for being here. Wish me luck! Oh great, here comes Shelly. I know I mentioned her to you in another episode. If you don't remember her, I'll just say this: she's my mortal enemy.

HEY, TY-SMELL.
HELLY, SMELL-EY, I DON'T HAVE TIME TO TALK TO YOU. I'M IN A HURRY.
REALLY? WHERE ARE YOU HEADED? TO TAKE A BATH?
VERY FUNNY. BUT IF YOU MUST KNOW—
I DON'T.
WELL, I'M TELLING YOU ANYWAY. I'M ON MY WAY TO GET A LEAD PART IN THE SIXTH-GRADE SHOW!
WHAT?! YOU?!

You see what I have to put up with? I can't wait to be onstage in the show so that I can prove to people like Smelly and Al how wrong they are and show everyone just how special I am. Okay, I've got to focus. My mom always says to take deep breaths when I'm feeling nervous. Here goes, breathe in . . . breathe out. Breathe in . . . breathe out. Breathe in . . .

BOOGIE! DID YOU JUST—
YUP, I FARTED!
WOW! AND I TOOK A DEEP BREATH OF IT! THAT'S HORRIBLE!

That's Mr. Attucks—he teaches theater here at school. I heard he was once in a movie or commercial or something, but I don't know for sure. He speaks really fancy, just like an actor. He calls everyone Mr. and Ms. and stuff. Anyway, he's pretty nice . . .

Pretty nice for a teacher that is. Okay, this is it. In a few minutes, I'll be up there shining like a diamond. I just need to relax, watch a few of the other kids—that'll probably calm me down. I'm sure some of them will be really good and a few of them will be terrible. I just hope I'm not one of the terrible ones. What if I am? I can't even think about it. I just need to sit here and breathe. Woo, I hope I'm not first! That would be horrible! Anything but first! Time to slide down in my seat so Mr. Attucks doesn't see my face until I want him to. That always works.

I'M GOING TO WAIT FOR QUIET...WAITING...WAITING... NO, MR. LACEY, YOU MAY NOT GO TO THE BATHROOM RIGHT NOW. I AM WAITING FOR SILENCE. YOU SHOULD'VE GONE BEFORE YOU CAME IN HERE. OKAY, NOW, WE CONTINUE OUR SEARCH FOR SILENCE AS WE ARE WAITING...WAITING...OKAY, THERE WE GO. NOW, WELCOME, STUDENTS, TO THE AUDITION FOR THIS YEAR'S SIXTH-GRADE SHOW. AS YOU KNOW, THIS YEAR'S THEME IS "NEW BEGINNINGS." IT IS THE SCHOOL'S HOPE THAT THE AUDITION PIECES YOU HAVE PREPARED FOR TODAY REFLECT YOUR POSITIVE HOPES AND DREAMS FOR YOUR FUTURES.

SEE? MY SONG IS PERFECT!
YES, MS. GREEN?
TYRELL IS BEHIND ME MUMBLING THINGS.
IS HE NOW? MR. EDWARDS, SINCE YOU CAN'T MAINTAIN SILENCE, I ASSUME YOU ARE READY TO COME UP HERE AND BE THE FIRST TO AUDITION.

THAT'S OKAY, YOU CAN LET SOMEONE ELSE GO.
NO, MR. EDWARDS, I INSIST.

HURRY, MR. EDWARDS. THERE ARE MANY OTHER STUDENTS WAITING QUIETLY FOR THEIR TURN. OH, MR. LACEY, YOU MAY GO TO THE BATHROOM NOW.
NO, THANK YOU, MR. ATTUCKS, I CAN HOLD IT.

Remember all that stuff I said about Mr. Attucks being nice? You can just forget that! Wow, I feel really sick. I think I'm going to sign off now because I don't think this is going to be pretty. Oh, if any of you know my mom's number, please call her and ask her to come pick me up after this. Thanks, talk to you later.

EPISODE THIRTEEN:
BRAIN FREEZE

Sooooo that was horrible. I'm sure you would like to hear about it, but if it's okay with you, I think I would rather talk about something else, like "brain freeze"—has that ever happened to you? Do you know what that is? It's when you have something to eat or drink that is really cold and you eat or drink it too fast. What happens is you get this strange pain in your head that makes you close your eyes and say to yourself, "What is going on?!" Kind of like my audition . . . I know I said I didn't want to talk about it, but if I'm being honest, I really can't think of anything else.

Okay, so where did I leave off in the last podcast? Oh yeah, the meanest teacher in the school, Mr. Attucks, was making me audition first. So there I was walking up to the stage. I was trying to stay calm and breathe like my mom had told me to do. The problem was I actually think I forgot to breathe, I was too busy looking at all the faces of the kids in my class. They were all just staring at me; some of them even looked like they were getting ready to laugh at me. They weren't actually laughing, but I could tell they were ready to. And then when I got onstage, all I could see was Shelly—she was whispering something to Rachel, and they were both looking at me and giggling. That really bothered me because, between you and me, I always kind of had a crush on Rachel, and there she was, whispering with my mortal enemy and giggling as they both watched me, waiting for me to fail. Then I remember looking away from them as I searched for a friendly face, only to find Boogie kind of smiling at me. I say "kind of" because I know Boogie, and by the way he was moving around in his seat, I think his face was saying, "Hurry up and sing, I reeeally have to pee."

I stood there for a little bit until finally Mr. Attucks told me to begin. I told everyone I was going to be performing my original song "Just Believe in Yourself," took one more deep breath, and opened my mouth and began to sing. At first, everyone was quiet, which was okay with me, but then a second later, everyone began to laugh. I was confused; I mean, I was there doing my best, singing my heart out, what was so funny? At that moment, I stopped being nervous, and I was able to focus on what I was actually doing. You ever stop in the middle of doing something weird and say to yourself, "What am I doing?" Like you're in class daydreaming as you draw in your notebook and then you kind of wake up, look down at your book, and say to yourself, "Why did I draw a monkey with a cell phone riding on a skateboard?" Well, that kind of happened to me. I woke up and realized that I was so nervous when I first started my audition that instead of singing my song, I had started singing that annoying song that Ricky was singing the other day! Remember?

Sippy sippy drink drink sippy sippy drink,
Red or blue or even pink,
When you're done with your sippy sippy drink,
Make sure you put it in the sink.

And if that wasn't bad enough, I wasn't even singing it very well. When I was done, Mr. Attucks was very angry. He told me I was "making a mockery of the auditions!" which I guess means he thinks I was making fun of him and the show, which I wasn't. Then he asked me to leave.

So here I am waiting for Boogie to get out of the bathroom. His mother is picking us up. Unfortunately, she's bringing Ricky with her. I'm really not in the mood for him, but she said she has some important news for us, which to me sounds really . . . important, I guess. Plus she said she's taking us to the park, which is always fun. After the audition I just had, I could use some fun. I really want you to meet Boogie's mom—she's pretty great. See you at the park.

EPISODE FOURTEEN:
LINK TAG

Okay, here's the situation, as bad as I feel about the audition, I don't have any time to talk to you about it because right now I am trying to hide from Boogie and his family. You see we're in a park near where me and Boogie live, and me, Boogie, Boogie's mom, and Ricky are playing Link Tag. You ever play that? It's really fun! The way you play it is someone starts out as "it," Boogie's mom was "it" at the beginning of our game. Anyway, if she tags you, you have to link arms with her so that you are kind of stuck to her, and then together the two of you try to tag someone else. If you tag someone else, they have to link up with you too. The game keeps going until everyone gets tagged and becomes part of the

link. In our game, Boogie's mom tagged Ricky first, of course, then they went after Boogie, who tried to run but tripped and fell, of course, and then they all linked up, and now the entire Lacey family is after me! It really is a lot of fun, mostly though because Boogie's mom has a way of making things fun. Uh-oh, here they come! Gotta run!

TEAM LACEY, GO RIGHT! NO, DEREK HONEY, YOUR OTHER RIGHT.
OH NO! I'M SO SORRY, MOMMY!
DEREK! YOU MADE MOMMY FALL DOWN!
MRS. LACEY!

THANK YOU SO MUCH, TYRELL, YOU'RE SUCH A GENTLEMAN. OH, AND BY THE WAY...
TAG!
GOT YOU!
BECAUSE OF ME, RIGHT, MOMMY?

I GUESS YOU COULD SAY THAT, BABY. BUT WE REALLY HAVE TO WORK ON THE DIFFERENCE BETWEEN YOUR LEFT AND RIGHT.
OKAY, BOYS, LET'S GO HOME AND HAVE A SNACK. ALSO, I NEED TO TALK TO YOU ABOUT SOMETHING VERY IMPORTANT.
MOMMY, MY LEG HURTS, I'VE GOT A BOO-BOO.
AW, MY SWEET LITTLE PRETTY RICKY. LEMME SEE THAT NASTY OLD BOO-BOO.

COME ON, BOYS, LET'S GO.
I WONDER WHAT YOUR MOM HAS TO TALK TO US ABOUT.
I WONDER WHAT SHE MADE US FOR A SNACK!
MOM! WHAT ARE WE GONNA EAT?

And that's Boogie's mom. I told you she was cool! Even on my saddest day ever, she can make me smile. She always plays games with us like that—she even plays video games . . . *video games*! And she's good! This was just what I needed. I was feeling really bad after that audition, and this made me feel a little better. When you're feeling bad, what are some things you do to cheer yourself up? For me I like to play games or talk to my family and friends, and sometimes, not every time but sometimes, those little things cheer me up.

Well, I'm going to go and get in Boogie's mom's minivan, but you don't have to come—trust me, you don't want to come. Right now me and Boogie are pretty sweaty, so we don't smell that great. And Ricky, well, to me he always smells kind of spoiled. Boogie's mom smells great as always though, kind of like flowers, but her nice smell is no match for our stink. I tell you what, I'll go in the van and hold my nose while you just blink yourself there. See you soon! On the count of three: one . . . two . . . three . . .

EPISODE FIFTEEN:
BLINDSIDED

What took you so long? I was starting to worry that you wouldn't make it. Boogie's mom hasn't told us her big news yet, but you did miss snacks! I wasn't really hungry, so I just had a banana. I love bananas—they taste great and just saying "banana" makes me laugh! Try it, say "banana" a bunch of times as quickly as you can. Go ahead, I'll wait . . . Did you do it? If you did, you know what I'm talking about. And if you didn't, I guess you're an apple person. Anyway, back to snacks, Ricky got his mom to give him a piece of the peach cobbler she made for dinner the other night. Her peach cobbler is delicious. And what did Boogie have?

you ask. Soup. Yup, he could've had anything, but he begged his mother for alphabet soup, that's the soup with letter-shaped noodles. And when his mom wasn't looking, he made me look at his bowl. He had spelled the word "POOP" with his noodles, and then he started laughing really hard. If I'm being honest, I think the only reason he asked for alphabet soup was so that he could spell out "POOP." Sometimes Boogie is just weird.

I KNOW YOU LIKE MY PEACH COBBLER. I WRAPPED UP THE REST OF IT AND IT'S ON THE KITCHEN COUNTER TO TAKE HOME FOR YOU AND YOUR FAMILY.
THANK YOU.

NOW, BOYS, I HAVE SOMETHING VERY IMPORTANT THAT I NEED TO SHARE WITH YOU. IN LIFE YOU MUST ALWAYS TRY TO DO WHAT'S BEST FOR YOU AND THE ONES YOU LOVE. FOR INSTANCE, DEREK BABY, WHAT IF YOU, YOUR BROTHER, AND TYRELL REALLY WANTED A TREAT AND I TOLD YOU THAT I HAD THREE TREATS IN ONE HAND AND ONLY ONE TREAT IN THE OTHER, WHICH ONE WOULD YOU CHOOSE?

THE ONE WITH THREE TREATS?
WHY?
BECAUSE THERE ARE THREE TREATS IN THAT HAND AND THERE ARE THREE OF US?
VERY GOOD, BABY. AND THAT'S KIND OF WHAT I WANT TO TALK TO YOU ABOUT...
SO CAN WE?
CAN YOU WHAT?
HAVE THE THREE TREATS?
BOOGIE THERE AREN'T THREE TREATS. YOUR MOM WAS JUST USING THAT AS AN EXAMPLE.
AWW, I KNEW I SHOULD'VE CHOSEN THE OTHER HAND.

YOU TWO ARE SUCH A GREAT TEAM! NOW BACK TO WHAT YOU SO BRILLIANTLY SAID, DEREK.
YOU PICKED THE HAND THAT WOULD BEST TAKE CARE OF THE NEEDS OF YOUR BROTHER, YOUR DEAR FRIEND, AND YOURSELF. RECENTLY I HAD TO MAKE A SIMILAR DECISION. I WAS OFFERED A JOB IN ANOTHER TOWN THAT WOULD PAY ME ENOUGH MONEY TO ENABLE ME TO BETTER TAKE CARE OF MY FAMILY.
YAY! CAN I HAVE A NEW VIDEO GAME?!
BOOGIE, YOU'RE NOT LISTENING.

SO DOES THAT MEAN YOU'RE MOVING AWAY?
MOVING?! WHO'S MOVING? ARE WE MOVING, MOMMY?
WHAT'S "MOVING"?
MY SWEET LITTLE PRETTY RICKY, "MOVING" IS GOING FROM ONE PLACE TO ANOTHER, AND YES, MY DEARS, IN SEARCH OF A BETTER LIFE WE WILL BE MOVING, BUT JUST KNOW THAT NO MATTER WHERE WE GO—
NO! I DON'T WANT TO MOVE!

OH NOW, SWEETIE...
HA-HA...
IT'S OKAY TO CRY.
NO, NO, DO NOT TEASE YOUR BROTHER. AND TAKE YOUR PLATE INTO THE KITCHEN RIGHT NOW.
sniff sniff
I'M VERY SAD TOO.

I'M GOING TO MISS THIS HOUSE. IT HAS SO MANY WONDERFUL MEMORIES OF ME WITH MY HUSBAND AND THE BOYS...AND OF COURSE *YOU.*
BUT I KNOW THAT THIS HOUSE DOES NOT OWN THOSE MEMORIES, I DO.
THEY LIVE HERE...
AND THEY LIVE HERE. AND NO ONE CAN TAKE THEM FROM US.
DO YOU REALLY HAVE TO GO?
YES, BUT ALWAYS KNOW, JUST LIKE THAT GAME OF LINK TAG WE PLAYED IN THE PARK, FROM THE DAY YOU AND DEREK MET IN KINDERGARTEN YOU WERE TAGGED BY THIS FAMILY, AND NO MATTER WHERE WE ALL ARE, WE WILL ALL FOREVER BE LINKED. COME HERE.

I LOVE YOU, TYRELL. I ASKED YOUR PARENTS IF I COULD TELL YOU AND DEREK AT THE SAME TIME. YOU TWO ARE SO SUPPORTIVE OF EACH OTHER AND I KNOW YOU'LL BOTH FIND A WAY TO BE THERE FOR EACH OTHER.
NOW, IF YOU WILL EXCUSE ME, I NEED TO GO AND TAKE CARE OF YOUR FRIEND. IF YOU CAN WAIT, I WILL DRIVE YOU HOME?
NO, THAT'S OKAY, I WOULD RATHER WALK.
OKAY, TYRELL HONEY. DON'T FORGET THE COBBLER, IT'S WRAPPED UP ON THE KITCHEN COUNTER.
BY THE WAY, I'M SORRY I FORGOT TO ASK. HOW DID THE AUDITION GO?
THE AUDITION? UM, FINE.

THAT'S GOOD TO HEAR. GET HOME SAFELY AND TELL YOUR PARENTS I SAID HI AND THAT I'LL CALL THEM TONIGHT.
CHOMP
CHOMP
CHOMP
CHOMP
WHAT ARE YOU DOING?!
CHOMP
CHOMP
I AM NOT GOING TO MISS HIM.

EPISODE SIXTEEN:
UM . . . YEAH

Hey, everyone. I'm not going to lie; it's been a while since I did an episode. I thought about doing one last week, but then I changed my mind. I don't know if you remember, but the last time I did an episode was the worst day of my life. I had a terrible audition, and then I found out that Boogie and his family are going to move away. And he's not moving away a long time from now when he and I are grown up and have our own cars and wives and stuff; he's moving at the end of this semester, pretty much right after the sixth-grade show . . . that I'm not in. Ever since I heard that, I haven't felt like doing anything, and that's why I haven't been doing my podcast. My parents have been talking to me and trying to cheer me up, but it hasn't worked, not even when my dad split his pants while we were doing a dance on TikTok . . . that was funny though—he split them right by his butt. Even Al has been acting a little nicer to me. Like the other morning I was in a hurry getting ready for school, so I was rushing. When I came downstairs for breakfast, Al noticed that I had put on two mismatched socks. Now, normally she would call me something like "Mismatchy Man" or "Mr. Mismatch" and then for some reason punch me really hard in the arm. But that day she just looked at me, told me to go back upstairs and change my socks, and then she said: *And the next time you see your weirdo other half, Boogie, tell him I actually kind of miss his potato head.*

And *then* she punched me. Like I said, she's been a little nicer to me, just a little.

Speaking of Boogie, he's been acting really strange. Al said she missed him because honestly he hasn't been coming around anymore. I mean I know he's sad and all, but he's been so not like . . . Boogie. It's like in this movie I saw where these space aliens came down and started capturing people and replacing them with fake space alien people that looked exactly like them.

I don't think that's what happened to Boogie, but he definitely seems like someone else. Like he's not funny, he doesn't laugh, really, he doesn't even smile. Boogie not smiling?

I know, strange, right? We really don't even speak that much anymore. We don't walk to school together anymore, we don't even go to see Monty together anymore. At first not seeing Boogie made me kind of sad, but now, if I'm being honest, I'm mad at Boogie. I mean, I'm not the one moving away—he is! I shouldn't have to make him feel better, he should have to make me feel better! Right?! Sorry, I'm yelling. You know what? I think I'm just going to stop talking about him. I am not going to mention his name anymore because it just makes me angry. I mean, how does he think it's okay to just move away and then not even say sorry? Nope, not gonna mention my former best friend's name anymore ever. And please, when you're around me, don't say his name either. Woo, thanks for listening! It felt great to finally talk about him, and I'm so glad I just decided to never say Boogie's name again. Okay, that last "Boogie" doesn't count because I was just saying "Boogie" to say that I will never say "Boogie" again. So now the no more saying "Boogie" promise officially starts . . . now!

EPISODE SEVENTEEN:
MONTY IN THE MIDDLE

Well, it's been two weeks and I haven't said you-know-who's name. Which is really tough because I would love to be able to talk to him about the whole me losing out on a part in the sixth-grade show disaster thing. Also, I reeeally wish I could talk to him about losing my BFF. But since he is the BFF I lost, I don't think that would make a lot of sense. Anyway, I've decided to do a few things to cheer myself up. First, I went and had a whole pizza, which if I'm being honest, from the sounds that my stomach is making, might have been a colossal mistake. But second, and more important, I'm here at the animal shelter to see my one true friend, Monty. I hope Monty isn't mad at me. I haven't been here in a long time, see, 'cause normally me and Boo—oops, almost said it. Yeah, well, normally me and someone you know would come here most days after school, but like I said before, I haven't been feeling like doing anything. But today I definitely feel like seeing my buddy Monty. Okay, I'm about to go inside. You don't have to leave though—I like having you with me. Come on in and see Monty!

AHHHH... MRS. WILSON, PLEASE SAVE ME!

NO, NO, CALI, YOU MUST NOT HURT DEREK.
IT IS SO NICE TO SEE THE TWO OF YOU BOYS; I KNOW THESE ANIMALS MISSED YOU AND SO DID I. COME ON, CALI—LET'S GET YOU BACK WITH YOUR FRIENDS.

HER NAME IS MRS. WILKINS, NOT MRS. WILSON.
I DON'T THINK YOU'RE RIGHT. YOU'RE NOT ALWAYS RIGHT YOU KNOW. SOMETIMES I'M RIGHT.
WELL, I'M RIGHT ABOUT THIS.
ARE YOU?

YES! YOU ARE THE ONE WHO IS SUPPOSED TO SAY SORRY!
TO MRS. WILSON?
IT'S *MRS. WILKINS,* AND, *NO,* TO *ME!*
WHY SHOULD I SAY SORRY TO YOU?!

BECAUSE YOU'RE LEAVING ME!
I DON'T WANT TO LEAVE! AND IF YOU WOULD EVER CALL ME OR TRY TO SPEAK TO ME WHEN YOU SEE ME AND ASK ME HOW I FEEL, I WOULD'VE TOLD YOU THAT! BUT NO, EVERY TIME YOU SEE ME, YOU TURN AND RUN. YOU DON'T THINK I SEE YOU, BUT I DO! IT'S LIKE YOU'RE AVOIDING ME, LIKE YOU DON'T WANT TO EVEN SAY MY NAME! HOW DO YOU THINK THAT MAKES ME FEEL?!
I...

BOOGIE... I'M SORRY.
I GUESS YOU SAW ALL THAT, MONTY. I REALLY MESSED THINGS UP, HUH? WHAT SHOULD I DO?
I DON'T THINK LICKING BOOGIE'S FACE IS A GOOD IDEA, BUT THANKS ANYWAY, MONTY.

EPISODE EIGHTEEN:
SOCIAL WORKING

So I have a day off from school. You would think I would get to sleep late and then go to the shelter and play all day with Monty, but NOPE. I have an assignment from school: I have to go to work with my parents. I mean I like spending time with my parents and all but not on my day off from school. Anyway, today my mom works from home so that should be easy, and then when dad goes to work, he said he would grab me and take me with him.

Right now I'm sitting near my mom and she is talking to a lady on the computer. She looks really old, like forty or eighty or something but really old. I think I told you before that my mom is a social worker, and the job of a social worker is to help people. The lady is telling my mom that she doesn't have enough money to pay her bills and no one to help her and take care of her. She sounds really sad, but my mom is saying things to her that look like they're making her feel better. My mom is telling the lady that she will find someone to come over and help take care of her, and she's also telling her not to worry so much about money. My mom is saying some other stuff, but I don't really understand it. Okay, the lady is thanking her now and my mom is hanging up.

TYRELL, IT IS IMPORTANT IN LIFE THAT WE TAKE THE TIME TO PUT OURSELVES IN OTHER PEOPLE'S POSITIONS, TO TRY TO SEE THE WORLD THROUGH THEIR EYES. IF YOU WERE HUNGRY AND THERE WAS NO ONE AROUND TO MAKE YOU A GRILLED CHEESE WITH OLIVES SANDWICH, HOW WOULD YOU FEEL?
HUNGRY, SAD, ANGRY?
EXACTLY. AND I BET YOU WOULD LIKE SOMEONE TO MAKE ONE FOR YOU AND MAYBE EVEN HELP YOU MAKE ONE.
NO OLIVES? BUT YOU LOVE WHEN I PUT OLIVES ON YOUR GRILLED CHEESE. RIGHT?
YES, BUT COULD THEY NOT PUT OLIVES ON IT?
OH, YES, I... I LOVE IT.

HMM, I THINK YOU'RE TELLING A LITTLE FIB SO AS NOT TO INSULT MY COOKING. YOU KNOW WHAT YOU DID THERE? YOU PUT YOURSELF IN MY PLACE AND THOUGHT ABOUT HOW I WOULD FEEL IF I HEARD THAT YOU DON'T LIKE OLIVES ON YOUR SANDWICH. WHAT YOU JUST PRACTICED IS SOMETHING CALLED "EMPATHY." THAT'S BIG-BOY STUFF.
WELL, I WISH I WOULD'VE KNOWN ABOUT THAT EMPILTY STUFF...
EMPATHY.
...EMPATHY STUFF THE OTHER DAY. I THINK I REALLY HURT BOOGIE'S FEELINGS.
BABY, NO MATTER HOW HARD WE TRY, WE WILL NEVER BE PERFECT. WE ALL MAKE MISTAKES AND SOMETIMES THOSE MISTAKES HURT THE PEOPLE CLOSE TO US.
HE'S REALLY MAD AT ME THOUGH.

HE MAY BE MAD NOW, BUT HE WON'T STAY MAD AT YOU.
YES, HE WILL. HE'S GOING TO BE MAD AT ME FOREVER.
"FOREVER" HUH? THAT'S A LONG TIME. HAVE YOU EVER BEEN MAD AT ME?
HUH?
YOU HEARD THE QUESTION— BE HONEST.
WELL, YEAH, KIND OF. THAT TIME YOU PUNISHED ME FOR USING YOUR BELT AND ONE OF YOUR SHOES TO MAKE A BATMAN CLIMBING ROPE.
WHY DID YOU NEED THE SHOE AGAIN?
TO BE LIKE THE HOOK TO GRAB THE TOP OF THE FENCE WHEN YOU CLIMB.

UMM-HMM... AND I GROUNDED YOU, NO TV AND NO INTERNET FOR TWO WEEKS?
AND YOU WERE REALLY MAD AT ME, RIGHT?
THREE.
VERY.
BUT DID YOU EVER STOP LOVING ME?
NO, MOMMY, NEVER!
MY ADVICE TO YOU: GO TO DEREK AND LISTEN TO HIM LIKE I LISTENED TO MRS. DAVIS. TRY TO SEE IF YOU CAN FIGURE OUT WHAT HE NEEDS AND ALSO WHAT YOU NEED AND THEN SEE IF THE TWO OF YOU CAN HELP EACH OTHER.

THANKS, YOU'RE A GREAT SOCIAL WORKER BUT AN EVEN BETTER MOM!

NOW, GO GET DRESSED. YOUR DAD SHOULD BE GETTING READY TO LEAVE FOR WORK SOON AND YOU DON'T WANT TO MAKE HIM LATE. OH, AND WE HAVE A SURPRISE FOR YOU.
CAN YOU TELL ME WHAT IT IS? OR EVEN A HINT.
IF I TOLD YOU, IT WOULDN'T BE A SURPRISE, WOULD IT? NOW, GET GOING AND HAVE A FUN DAY WITH YOUR DAD!

EPISODE NINETEEN:
BUS DRIVING

If I'm being honest, my mom's job was way more interesting then I thought it would be. Now I'm with my dad, and I already know his job is very cool—he is a bus driver. Right now we are walking around the bus that he is about to drive. He says we are doing this so that we can make sure it is safe for us and his passengers to ride in. I don't know exactly what he is looking for, but he definitely looks very serious. The only time he has smiled was when he kicked one of the tires and then I kicked it too. He laughed at that, and even though I hurt my toe when I did it, I just laughed, too, and didn't even tell him about my toe because I didn't want to ruin the moment.

Now we're on the bus and my father is sitting in the bus driver's seat. He is staring down at all the things in front of him. I don't know what he's doing exactly, but he looks really smart.

YES, AND IT IS IMPORTANT THAT I KNOW HOW THIS BUS IS FEELING IF I'M GOING TO ASK IT TO HELP ME CARRY MY PASSENGERS SAFELY.
HOW DO YOU ASK IT?
YOU SEE THAT KEY? I WANT YOU TO TURN IT. IF THE BUS STARTS, THAT MEANS IT'S READY TO GO. IF IT DOESN'T, THAT MEANS IT NEEDS SOME ASSISTANCE. GO AHEAD, TURN THE KEY AND LET'S SEE WHAT HAPPENS.
WHY DIDN'T IT START? WHAT'S WRONG?
JUST LIKE HOW SOMETIMES YOU NEED A LITTLE ENCOURAGEMENT FROM ME OR YOUR MOTHER WHEN YOU WAKE UP IN THE MORNING FOR SCHOOL, I THINK THIS BUS COULD USE A LITTLE HELP FROM US. LET'S TRY AGAIN, ONLY THIS TIME I'M GOING TO PRESS ON THE PEDAL AND GIVE IT SOME GAS AS WE BOTH ASK HER NICELY TO START.

WHAT'S HER NAME?
BESSIE...BESSIE BUS. ON THE COUNT OF THREE, TURN THE KEY AND LET'S ASK BESSIE BUS TO PLEASE START. ONE...TWO... THREE!
COME ON, BESSIE! BESSIE BUS, PLEASE START!

GREAT WORK, HIGH SPEED!
I CAN'T BELIEVE IT WORKED!
OF COURSE IT DID. AND DO YOU KNOW WHY?
BECAUSE WE YELLED OUT HER NAME?

BECAUSE YOU ENCOURAGED HER, YOU SUPPORTED HER, AND EVEN BEFORE ALL OF THAT WE CHECKED IN WITH HER TO SEE HOW SHE WAS FEELING. THAT'S SOMETHING I ALWAYS WANT YOU TO REMEMBER TO DO. LIKE TODAY ON THE BUS, I WANT YOU TO SIT IN THE SEAT RIGHT OVER THERE WHERE I CAN SEE YOU, BUT IF YOU SEE SOMEONE WHO YOU CAN TELL REALLY NEEDS THAT SEAT, I WANT YOU TO OFFER IT TO THEM. OKAY?
OF COURSE, DAD, BECAUSE I'M PRACTICING EMPATHY.

IT'S BIG-BOY STUFF.
WOW, HIGH SPEED, HOW DO YOU KNOW THAT?
HA! THAT IT IS! BY DOING THAT YOU'LL ALSO BE PRACTICING SOME OTHER BIG-BOY STUFF LIKE GENEROSITY AND COMPASSION!

NICE! HEY, DAD, MOM SAID THE TWO OF YOU HAVE A SURPRISE FOR ME? CAN YOU TELL ME WHAT IT IS?
OH NO, WE DON'T NEED YOUR MOM GETTING MAD AT US.

SHE WOULDN'T STAY MAD AT US FOREVER.
SHE WOULDN'T STAY MAD AT YOU. ME, THAT'S ANOTHER STORY. NOW PUSH THAT HORN THERE IN THE MIDDLE OF THE STEERING WHEEL AND LET'S GET MOVING!
BAAAAAH!

EPISODE TWENTY:
BOOGIE DOWN

Hey, everyone, welcome back! Today is my favorite day of the week—Saturday! Why? you ask. You've got to be kidding me! No school! Don't get me wrong, I like school, but I like Saturdays even more. Today isn't just any Saturday episode though—today I have a special guest! Guess who it is!

He said hi, and if you guessed Monty, you were right! Now I know Monty has been on my show before but not like this. Right now I'm not at the shelter with Monty—I'm walking in the park near my house with him. Wanna know why? We adopted him! Remember the surprise my parents said they had for me in the last episode? Monty was it! He's the best surprise ever! After work that day, my dad asked me if I wanted to go to the shelter and visit Monty, and I was like, "Ah-yeah!" Actually I said, "Yes, Dad," 'cause I don't think he would've liked me saying "Ah-yeah." Anyway, when we got there, Mom was there, too, and, well, this happened.

WE WANT YOU TO KNOW THAT WE ALWAYS SEE YOU. AND THOSE TIMES IN YOUR LIFE WHEN YOU HAVE STRUGGLES YOU ARE NEVER ALONE.
OKAY, YOU'RE BOTH ACTING A LITTLE WEIRD. WHY ARE YOU TELLING ME THIS AT THE SHELTER? AND REALLY, MOM, WHY ARE YOU HERE?

LITTLE BOY, I AM A MOM AND I HAVE THE POWER TO SHOW UP ANYWHERE I WANT, WHEN YOU LEAST EXPECT IT.
WELL, THAT JUST SOUNDS SCARY.

I HAVE WIFE POWERS TOO.
I SEE WHAT YOU MEAN, HIGH SPEED.
BUT IN ANSWER TO YOUR QUESTION, SWEETIE, YOUR FATHER AND I HAVE NOTICED HOW DOWN YOU'VE BEEN SO WE THOUGHT IT WOULD BE A GOOD IDEA IF I CAME HERE TO THE SHELTER TO ASK ONE OF YOUR DEAREST FRIENDS WHAT WE SHOULD DO ABOUT IT.
YOU SPOKE TO MRS. WILKINS? I MEAN SHE'S NICE AND ALL BUT I WOULDN'T CALL HER A CLOSE FRIEND.
BOY, WHAT IS WRONG WITH YOU? NO, I SPOKE WITH MONTY. AND AFTER A REALLY GOOD CONVERSATION, HE SUGGESTED...

Then Mrs. Wilkins said goodbye to Monty and thanked us for adopting him and giving him a new loving home. Since then I've been spending a lot of time with Monty. My parents told me that he's my responsibility, which is fine by me, so he kind of comes with me everywhere. He even sleeps with me sometimes—only don't tell my mom because she doesn't like him being on my bed. Right now me and Monty are going for a walk in the park so that he can poop. My mom said that's one of the responsibilities I have with Monty, but I don't mind going with him. He comes with me to the bathroom when I go, so I figure it's only fair. Only difference is when he has to go I have to clean up after him, but when I go, he just kind of stares at me.

Monty has really made me think about my last year at MGE. I thought getting a part in the sixth-grade show was the most important thing ever . . . until I lost my best friend. The worst part about it is I feel like it's all my fault. I shouldn't have blamed Boogie for moving away—his mom is only trying to do what's best for their family. And I should've asked Boogie how he was feeling. He always does that for me; he's always there for me. Like at the audition, I know he had to go to the bathroom really badly, but he didn't—he stayed for me. And when I looked out and saw all those faces laughing at me, there was one face that wasn't—Boogie. I wish I could apologize to him, but when he sees me he runs, just like what I was doing to him. I don't think he'll ever speak to me again. I guess Monty will have to be my BFF.

WHAT'S WRONG, MONTY? DO YOU SEE A SQUIRREL?
RUFF RUFF RUFF!
WHOA, MONTY! SLOW DOWN!! YOU'RE GONNA MAKE ME FALL!
BOOGIE?!
TYRELL?!
RUFF!

MONTY, LOOK OUT!!!
THANK YOU, MONTY, BUT YOUR BREATH IS TERRIBLE!
WELL, HE WAS JUST LICKING HIS BUTT!
OH, NO! GET OFF ME, MONTY!

BOOGIE, I'M SORRY, SO SORRY!
I KNEW IT! I TOLD YOU HER NAME WAS MRS. WILSON.
HER NAME IS MRS. WILKINS AND, NO, THAT'S NOT WHAT I'M TALKING ABOUT.
THEN WHAT ARE YOU SORRY FOR?
THE WAY I'VE BEEN TREATING YOU! I THOUGHT I WAS MAD AT YOU BECAUSE YOU WERE LEAVING ME, BUT REALLY I WAS JUST SAD BECAUSE YOU HAVE TO MOVE AWAY. YOU'RE MY BEST FRIEND! IF I'M BEING HONEST, YOU'RE THE BEST FRIEND ANYONE COULD EVER HAVE! AND I SHOULD'VE THOUGHT ABOUT YOUR FEELINGS. I SHOULD'VE ASKED YOU IF THERE WAS ANYTHING I COULD DO TO MAKE YOU FEEL BETTER.

THANK YOU. I HAVE FELT REALLY LONELY WITHOUT YOU.
ME TOO. I KNOW YOU'RE PROBABLY STILL PRETTY MAD AT ME, BUT DO YOU THINK YOU'LL EVER BE ABLE TO FORGIVE ME?
HMM, LET ME THINK ABOUT IT.
HEY?! DID YOU JUST FART?
THE ANSWER TO BOTH OF YOUR QUESTIONS IS YES.

GOOD AFTERNOON, BOYS.
HELLO, MR. ATTUCKS. WHAT ARE YOU DOING OUT OF SCHOOL?
TEACHERS DO HAVE LIVES YOU KNOW. ANYWAY, I WAS WALKING THROUGH THE PARK AND I NOTICED THE TWO OF YOU PLAYING WITH THAT ADORABLE DOG. DOES HE BELONG TO EITHER ONE OF YOU?
HE'S MINE. DID HE DO SOMETHING WRONG. IF HE DID, I'M VERY SORRY.
NO, QUITE THE OPPOSITE. AS YOU MAY HAVE HEARD, QUENTIN AND LISA BOTH CAME DOWN WITH THE CHICKEN POX. WHICH IS VERY UNFORTUNATE FOR THEM AND EVEN MORE FOR THE SHOW, FOR YOU SEE THEY ALONG WITH THEIR DOG WERE SET TO PARTICIPATE IN IT. WITH THAT SAID, I WOULD LIKE TO OFFER YOU BOYS AND YOUR LOVELY DOG—
MONTY.

MONTY...ROLES IN THIS YEAR'S PAGEANT. NOW IF YOU WOULD LIKE TO DO IT, I WILL NEED A PERMISSION SLIP FROM YOUR PARENTS ASAP. ARE YOU INTERESTED?
YES, WE ARE!
EXCELLENT! AND MR. EDWARDS, NO "SIPPY CUP" AND MR. LACEY, MAKE SURE YOU GO TO THE BATHROOM BEFORE YOU GET ONSTAGE. GOOD AFTERNOON, BOYS.

And that's why I love Saturdays, especially this one! I got a part in the show, but even better than that, I got my best friend back! Talk to you soon!

EPISODE TWENTY-ONE:
THE BIG FINALE

Hey, everyone, and welcome to my final show of the semester! Today was the last day of school, and now we get to go on a semester break. For as much as I might have complained about school, and, well, I guess about pretty much everything else, if I'm being honest, this semester turned out really great! Now let's see, where did I leave things off with all of you? Oh yeah, in the park! Sorry I haven't done a show since then, but I was, I mean we were, very busy getting ready for the show. And when I say "we," I mean me, Boogie, and Monty. Since that day, the three of us have spent all our time together, except when we're sleeping of course, but even then, since he's going to be moving away soon,

Boogie's mom has let him spend the night a lot. Al is sick of Boogie again, but it's really fun having him sleep over even if he does snore like a baby bear.

As for the show, it went really well! Sorry I didn't invite you, but I didn't want to make a big deal out of it and get myself nervous and stuff. I just wanted it to be fun, and being onstage with my two best friends made that really easy. Mr. Attucks gave us the roles of farmers and Monty got to be our pig. We were supposed to be farmers who were planting crops for the future—a little lame if you ask me—but I'm not complaining; we had a blast. And even though we each had only one line and Boogie accidentally stepped on the back of my boot, which made us fall backward and knock down Joelle, Jabril, and Andre, who were dressed up as cornstalks, which then got Monty excited and caused him to run over to the cornstalks, lift up his leg, and start to pee, which made an auditorium full of kids and parents scream, "Ewwww!" and Mr. Attucks dove onto the stage and stopped him before he could actually pee . . . I think the show was a huge and hysterical success!

Right now me and Boogie and our families are at my house getting ready to have a big dinner to celebrate how well we did in the show. I'm excited for this but a little sad because Boogie is actually moving next week during the semester break, so this might be like our last dinner together. When I say "last dinner" though, I don't mean like last forever—I just mean for a while. After talking to Boogie and his mom and my parents, I have realized that just because someone is far away doesn't mean you can't stay in touch. We can write, text, talk on the phone, and maybe even visit each other sometimes. I know that's not as easy as just going over to his house or seeing him in school, but Boogie is like my brother, so I know things will work out. Anyway, all that performing onstage has got me reeeally hungry, and since Boogie's mom did a lot of the cooking, I can't wait to eat. Sorry, Mom! Dinners with our families together are always fun so I'm gonna leave my brain microphone on so you can hear. Meet you at the table!

FINALLY, HIGH SPEED! OKAY, NOW WE'RE GONNA NEED YOU AND DEREK TO STAND UP, PLEASE.
LET'S HEAR IT FOR TODAY'S TWO BIG STARS!
MONTY! DON'T FORGET ABOUT MONTY. HE WAS A PART OF THE SHOW TOO!
A PART OF THE SHOW? MONTY STOLE THE SHOW!
BOY, I TOLD YOU TO WALK HIM BEFORE THE PAGEANT.

NOW, KIDS—DEREK, LITTLE RICKY, ALEXANDRA, TYRELL—AS YOU KNOW THIS MEAL IS TO HONOR ALL YOUR ACCOMPLISHMENTS THIS SEMESTER. I KNOW I SPEAK FOR ALL THE ADULTS IN THIS ROOM WHEN I SAY I'M PROUD OF ALL YOUR HARD WORK. I KNOW IT'S NOT EASY BEING A YOUNG PERSON THESE DAYS, BUT I WANT YOU TO KNOW WE SEE YOU AND YOUR EFFORTS AND WE APPRECIATE AND LOVE YOU.
AND WHILE THIS DINNER IS TO CELEBRATE YOU KIDS, WE ALSO WANTED TO USE IT TO WISH OUR DEAR FRIENDS, THE LACEYS, WELL WITH THEIR MOVE AND TO LET THEM KNOW WE LOVE THEM AND WILL MISS THEM.
AW, THANK YOU! AND WE LOVE YOU TOO! ARE YOU GOING TO TELL THEM NOW, CHARLENE?

TELL US WHAT, MOM?
WELL, WE'VE ALL AGREED THAT ONCE THE LACEYS GET SETTLED, TYRELL, YOU CAN GO AND STAY WITH THEM FOR TWO WEEKS TO HELP DEREK GET ACCUSTOMED TO HIS NEW SURROUNDINGS. BUT YOU BOTH HAVE TO PROMISE TO BEHAVE AND STAY OUT OF TROUBLE.
YOU BOYS PROMISE?
WE PROMISE! WE PROMISE!
WHAT ABOUT MONTY? CAN HE COME?
IRIS, I KNOW YOU'LL BE VERY BUSY WITH THE MOVE. TYRELL HONEY, I THINK MONTY CAN WAIT UNTIL THE NEXT TRIP.
AW NO, THAT'S ALL RIGHT. HE CAN COME. HE'S FAMILY.

THANK YOU, MRS. LACEY! AND WHAT DO YOU SAY, MONTY?
HE CAN. COME ON, MONTY, DON'T BE RUDE. WHAT DO YOU SAY TO MRS. LACEY?
YOU AND THAT DOG. YOU KNOW TYRELL SAYS HE CAN TALK.
THANKS!

EPISODE TWENTY-TWO:
END CREDITS SCENE

Hey, everyone, welcome to the end credits scene—you know, like how at the end of an action movie, after all that boring stuff where people's names go by, there's always, like, this extra scene? Well, that's what this is! I'm about to tell Boogie something, and I wanted you all to be here for it.

MONTY TALKED?! THAT WAS INCREDIBLE!
FOR WHAT?
I TOLD YOU HE COULD! NOW, GET READY.
WE'VE GOT TO END THE SHOW. HELLO, EVERYONE, I'M TYRELL AND THIS IS MY SIDEKICK, BOOGIE...
SIDEKICK? REALLY?
YEAH... FOR NOW.
BEST SEMESTER EVER!
AND THIS IS *THE TYRELL SHOW*—SIGNING OFF!
BYE!
BYE!